THE
ICE OWL

A novella by

CAROLYN IVES GILMAN

PHOENIX PICK BOOKLETS

an imprint of

ARC
MANOR
Rockville, Maryland

ISBN: 978-1-61242-110-0

www.PhoenixPick.com
Great Science Fiction at Great Prices

Published by Phoenix Pick
an imprint of Arc Manor
P. O. Box 10339
Rockville, MD 20849-0339
www.ArcManor.com

Introduction

The Ice Owl is set in the same universe—though not on the same planet— as my previous novella from Arc Manor/Phoenix Pick, *Arkfall*. I have started calling this universe the Twenty Planets. I never planned to write linked stories; this universe just keeps luring me back because the rules are congenial. Humans have invented light-speed transport and (by the time this story takes place) primitive instantaneous communication. This creates some interesting situations I like to play with. For example, in this story I wanted to explore what it would be like to grow up as an interplanetary vagabond—a childhood similar to what military kids have today, but with the time delays of space travel built in.

The setting of this story is based on a type of planet found in our own solar system—a tidally locked planet like Mercury, where one face is permanently turned toward the sun, making half the planet too hot to inhabit and the other half too cold. Life would only be feasible in the narrow strip between permanent day and permanent night. Such a planet is unlikely to have an atmosphere, so my city had to be domed. The inhabitants would have plenty of solar and geothermal energy, so they could get their oxygen from the iron oxides that are plentiful on this planet, and use the iron for building. Living in an iron city on an airless planet seemed a rather grim and desperate existence to me, so I gave them a grim and desperate culture. Fundamentalist religion, authoritarian power structures, and extremism are all reactions to the sheer difficulty of surviving in a place like this.

The plot of *The Ice Owl* revolves around an experience just about everyone has had—the moment when you realize that the adults you have grown up with are not really any wiser, more powerful, or more competent at life than you are. I remember how disillusioned I felt when I found that my parents were just muddling along, and didn't really know any more about coping with the world than I did. It takes a long time to forgive them for that.

This is also a story about the moment when you first realize that life is a series of deliberate choices for which you are going to be responsible.

When we are children, all the important choices are made for us by adults. We might not like this, but at least the onus of deciding is out of our hands. But that phase of life ends. I am frustrated by how many stories indulge in the wish-fulfillment fantasy of a life that is guided by outside forces. Think of all the stories where the protagonist is fated to become king, or to save the world, or is thrust into a situation where there is only one right course of action. These stories satisfy our longing for a return to an infantile existence. But life is not like that. We aren't just acted upon by events; we have to create our own futures through our own decisions, for better or worse. What's more, we create other people's futures.

Twice a day, stillness settled over the iron city of Glory to God as the citizens turned west and waited for the world to ring. For a few moments the motionless red sun on the horizon, half-concealed by the western mountains, lit every face in the city: the just-born and the dying, the prisoners and the veiled, the devout and the profane. The sound started so low it could only be heard by the bones; but as the moments passed the metal city itself began to ring in sympathetic harmony, till the sound resolved into a note—The Note, priests said, sung by the heart of God to set creation going. Its vibratory mathematics embodied all structure; its pitch implied all scales and chords; its beauty was the ovum of all devotion and all faithlessness. Nothing more than a note was needed to extrapolate the universe.

The Note came regular as clockwork, the only timebound thing in a city of perpetual sunset.

On a ledge outside a window in the rustiest part of town, crouched one of the ominous cast-iron gargoyles fancied by the architects of Glory to God—or so it seemed until it moved. Then it resolved into an adolescent girl dressed all in black. Her face was turned west, her eyes closed in a look of private exaltation as The Note reverberated through her. It was a face that had just recently lost the chubbiness of childhood, so that the clean-boned adult was beginning to show through. Her name, also a recent development, was Thorn. She had chosen it because it evoked suffering and redemption.

As the bell tones whispered away, Thorn opened her eyes. The city before her was a composition in red and black: red of the sun and the dust-plain outside the girders of the dome; black of the shadows and the works of mankind. Glory to God was built against the cliff of an old crater and rose in stair steps of fluted pillars and wrought arches till the towers of the Protectorate grazed the underside of the dome where it met the cliff face. Behind the distant, glowing windows of the palaces, twined with iron ivy, the priest-magistrates and executives lived unimaginable lives—though Thorn still pictured them looking down on all the rest of the city, on the smelteries and temples, the warring neighborhoods ruled by militias, the veiled women, and at the very bottom, befitting its status, the Waster enclave where unrepentant immigrants like Thorn and her mother lived, sunk in a bath of sin. The Waste was not truly of the city, except as a perennial itch in its flesh. The Godly said it was the sin, not the oxygen, that rusted everything in the Waste. A man who came home with a red smudge on his clothes might as well have been branded with the address.

Thorn's objection to her neighborhood lay not in its sin, which did not live up to its reputation, but its inauthenticity. From her rooftop perch she looked down on its twisted warrens full of coffee shops, underground publishers, money launderers, embassies, tattoo parlors, and art galleries. This was the ninth planet she had lived on in her short life, but in truth she had never left her native culture, for on every planet the Waster enclaves were the same. They were always a mother lode of contraband ideas. Everywhere, the expatriate intellectuals of the Waste were regarded as exotic and dangerous, the vectors of infectious transgalactic ideas—but lately, Thorn had begun to find them pretentious and phony. They were rooted nowhere, pieces of cultural bricolage. Nothing reached to the core; it was all veneer, just like the rust.

Outside, now—she looked past the spiked gates into Glory to God proper—there lay dark desires and age-old hatreds, belief so unexamined it permeated every tissue like a marinade. The natives had not chosen their beliefs; they had inherited them, breathed them in with the iron dust in their first breath. Their struggles were authentic ones.

Her eyes narrowed as she spotted movement near the gate. She was, after all, on lookout duty. There seemed to be more than the usual traffic this afternote, and the cluster of young men by the gate did not look furtive enough to belong. She studied them through her pocket binoculars and saw a telltale flash of white beneath one long coat. White, the color of the uncorrupted.

She slipped back through the gable window into her attic room, then down the iron spiral staircase at the core of the vertical tower apartment. Past the fifth-floor closets and the fourth-floor bedrooms she went, to the third-floor offices. There she knocked sharply on one of the molded sheet-iron doors. Within, there was a thump, and in a moment Maya cracked it open enough to show one eye.

"There's a troop of Incorruptibles by the gate," Thorn said.

Inside the office, a woman's voice gave a frightened exclamation. Thorn's mother turned and said in her fractured version of the local tongue, "Worry not yourself. We make safely go." She then said to Thorn, "Make sure the bottom door is locked. If they come, stall them."

Thorn spun down the stair like a black tornado, past the living rooms to the kitchen on street level. The door was locked, but she unlocked it to peer out. The alarm was spreading down the street. She watched signs being snatched from windows, awnings rolled up, and metal grills rumbling down across storefronts. The crowds that always pressed from curb to curb this time of day had vanished. Soon the stillness of impending storm settled over the street. Then Thorn heard the faraway chanting, like premonitory thunder. She closed and locked the door.

Maya showed up, looking rumpled, her lovely honey-gold hair in ringlets. Thorn said, "Did you get her out?" Maya nodded. One of the main appeals of this apartment had been the hidden escape route for smuggling out Maya's clients in emergencies like this.

On this planet, as on the eight before, Maya earned her living in the risky profession of providing reproductive services. Every planet was different, it seemed, except that on all of them women wanted something that was forbidden. What they wanted varied: here, it was babies. Maya did a brisk business in contraband semen and embryos for women who needed to become pregnant without their infertile husbands guessing how it had been accomplished.

The chanting grew louder, harsh male voices in unison. They watched together out the small kitchen window. Soon they could see the approaching wall of men dressed in white, marching in lockstep. The army of righteousness came even with the door, then passed by. Thorn and Maya exchanged a look of mutual congratulation and locked little fingers in their secret handshake. Once again, they had escaped.

Thorn opened the door and looked after the army. An assortment of children was tagging after them, so Maya said, "Go see what they're up to."

The Incorruptibles had passed half a dozen potential targets by now: the bank, the musical instrument store, the news service, the sex shop. They didn't pause until they came to the small park that lay in the center of an intersection. Then the phalanx lined up opposite the school. With military precision, some of them broke the bottom windows and others lit incendiary bombs and tossed them in. They waited to make sure the blaze was started, then gave a simultaneous shout and marched away, taking a different route back to the gate.

They had barely left when the Protectorate fire service came roaring down the street to put out the blaze. This was not, Thorn knew, out of respect for the school or for the Waste, which could have gone up in flame wholesale for all the authorities cared; it was simply that in a domed city, a fire anywhere was a fire everywhere. Even the palaces would have to smell the smoke and clean up soot if it were not doused quickly. Setting a fire was as much a defiance of the Protectorate as of the Wasters.

Thorn watched long enough to know that the conflagration would not spread, and then walked back home. When she arrived, three women were sitting with Maya at the kitchen table. Two of them Thorn knew: Clarity and Bick, interstellar wanderers whose paths had crossed Thorn's and Maya's on two previous planets. The first time, they had been feckless coeds; the second time, seasoned adventurers. They were past middle age now, and had become the most sensible people Thorn had ever met. She had seen them face insurrection and exile with genial good humor and a canister of tea.

Right now their teapot was filling the kitchen with a smoky aroma, so Thorn fished a mug out of the sink to help herself. Maya said, "So what were the Incorruptibles doing?"

"Burning the school," Thorn said in a seen-it-all-before tone. She glanced at the third visitor, a stranger. The woman had a look of time-shock that gave her away as a recent arrival in Glory to God via lightbeam from another planet. She was still suffering from the temporal whiplash of waking up ten or twenty years from the time she had last drawn breath.

"Annick, this is Thorn, Maya's daughter," Clarity said. She was the talkative, energetic one of the pair; Bick was the silent, steady one.

"Hi," Thorn said. "Welcome to the site of Creation."

"Why were they burning the school?" Annick said, clearly distressed by the idea. She had pale eyes and a soft, gentle face. Thorn made a snap judgment: Annick was not going to last long here.

"Because it's a vector of degeneracy," Thorn said. She had learned the phrase from Maya's current boyfriend, Hunter.

"What has happened to this planet?" Annick said. "When I set out it was isolated, but not regressive."

They all made sympathetic noises, because everyone at the table had experienced something similar. Lightbeam travel was as fast as the universe allowed, but even the speed of light had a limit. Planets inevitably changed during transit, not always for the better. "Waster's luck," Maya said fatalistically.

Clarity said, "The Incorruptibles are actually a pretty new movement. It started among the conservative academics and their students, but they have a large following now. They stand against the graft and nepotism of the Protectorate. People in the city are really fed up with being harassed by policemen looking for bribes, and corrupt officials who make up new fees for everything. So they support a movement that promises to kick the grafters out and give them a little harsh justice. Only it's bad news for us."

"Why?" Annick said. "Wouldn't an honest government benefit everyone?"

"You'd think so. But honest governments are always more intrusive. You can buy toleration and personal freedom from a corrupt government. The Protectorate leaves this Waster enclave alone because it brings them profit. If the Incorruptibles came into power, they'd have to bow to public opinion and exile us, or make us conform. The general populace is pretty isolationist. They think our sin industry is helping keep the Protectorate in power. They're right, actually."

"What a Devil's bargain," Annick said.

They all nodded. Waster life was full of irony.

"What's Thorn going to do for schooling now?" Clarity asked Maya.

Maya clearly hadn't thought about it. "They'll figure something out," she said vaguely.

Just then Thorn heard Hunter's footsteps on the iron stairs, and she said to annoy him, "I could help Hunter."

"Help me do what?" Hunter said as he descended into the kitchen. He was a lean and angle-faced man with square glasses and a small goatee. He always dressed in black and could not speak without sounding sarcastic. Thorn thought he was a poser.

"Help you find Gmintas, of course," Thorn said. "That's what you do."

He went over to the Turkish coffee machine to brew some of the bitter, hyperstimulant liquid he was addicted to. "Why can't you go to school?" he said.

"They burned it down."

"Who did?"

"The Incorruptibles. Didn't you hear them chanting?"

"I was in my office."

He was always in his office. It was a mystery to Thorn how he was going to locate any Gminta criminals when he disdained going out and mingling with people. She had once asked Maya, "Has he ever actually caught a Gminta?" and Maya had answered, "I hope not."

All in all, though, he was an improvement over Maya's last boyfriend, who had absconded with every penny of savings they had. Hunter at least had money, though where it came from was a mystery.

"I could be your field agent," Thorn said.

"You need an education, Thorn," Clarity said.

"Yes," Hunter agreed. "If you knew something, you might be a little less annoying."

"People like you give education a bad name," Thorn retorted.

"Stop being a brat, Tuppence," Maya said.

"That's not my name anymore!"

"If you act like a baby, I'll call you by your baby name."

"You always take his side."

"You could find her a tutor," Clarity said. She was not going to give up.

"Right," Hunter said, sipping inky liquid from a tiny cup. "Why don't you ask one of those old fellows who play chess in the park?"

"They're probably all pedophiles!" Thorn said in disgust.

"On second thought, maybe it's better to keep her ignorant," Hunter said, heading up the stairs again.

"I'll ask around and see who's doing tutoring," Clarity offered.

"Sure, okay," Maya said noncommittally.

Thorn got up, glowering at their lack of respect for her independence and self-determination. "I am captain of my own destiny," she announced, then made a strategic withdrawal to her room.

***

The next forenote Thorn came down from her room in the face-masking veil that women of Glory to God all wore, outside the Waste. When Maya saw her, she said, "Where are you going in that getup?"

"Out," Thorn said.

In a tone diluted with real worry, Maya said, "I don't want you going into the city, Tup."

Thorn was icily silent till Maya said, "Sorry—Thorn. But I still don't want you going into the city."

"I won't," Thorn said.

"Then what are you wearing that veil for? It's a symbol of bondage."

"Bondage to God," Thorn said loftily.

"You don't believe in God."

Right then Thorn decided that she would.

When she left the house and turned toward the park, the triviality of her home and family fell away like lint. After a block, she felt transformed. Putting on the veil had started as a simple act of rebellion, but out in the street it became far more. Catching her reflection in a shop window, she felt disguised in mystery. The veil intensified the imagined face it concealed, while exoticizing the eyes it revealed. She had become something shadowy, hidden. The Wasters all around her were obsessed with their own surfaces, with manipulating what they *seemed* to be. All depth, all that was earnest, withered in the acid of their inauthenticity. But with the veil on, Thorn *had* no surface, so she was immune. What lay behind the veil was negotiated, contingent, rendered deep by suggestion.

In the tiny triangular park in front of the blackened shell of the school, life went on as if nothing had changed. The tower fans turned lazily, creating a pleasant breeze tinged a little with soot. Under their strutwork shadows, two people walked little dogs on leashes, and the old men bent over their chessboards. Thorn scanned the scene through the slit in her veil, then walked toward a bench where an old man sat reading from an electronic slate.

She sat down on the bench. The old man did not acknowledge her presence, though a watchful twitch of his eyebrow told her he knew she was there. She had often seen him in the park, dressed impeccably in threadbare suits of a style long gone. He had an oblong, drooping face and big hands that looked as if they might once have done clever things. Thorn sat considering what to say.

"Well?" the old man said without looking up from his book. "What is it you want?"

Thorn could think of nothing intelligent to say, so she said, "Are you a historian?"

He lowered the slate. "Only in the sense that we all are, us Wasters. Why do you want to know?"

"My school burned down," Thorn said. "I need to find a tutor."

"I don't teach children," the old man said, turning back to his book.

"I'm not a child!" Thorn said, offended.

He didn't look up. "Really? I thought that's what you were trying to hide, behind that veil."

She took it off. At first he paid no attention. Then at last he glanced up indifferently, but saw something that made him frown. "You are the child that lives with the Gminta hunter."

His cold tone made her feel defensive on Hunter's behalf. "He doesn't hunt all Gmintas," she said, "just the wicked ones who committed the Holocide. The ones who deserve to be hunted."

"What do you know about the Gmintan Holocide?" the old man said with withering dismissal.

Thorn smiled triumphantly. "I was there."

He stopped pretending to read and looked at her with bristly disapproval. "How could you have been there?" he said. "It happened 141 years ago."

"I'm 145 years old, sequential time," Thorn said. "I was 37 when I was five, and 98 when I was seven, and 126 when I was twelve." She enjoyed shocking people with this litany.

"Why have you moved so much?"

"My mother got pregnant without my father's consent, and when she refused to have an abortion he sued her for copyright infringement. She'd made unauthorized use of his genes, you see. So she ducked out to avoid paying royalties, and we've been on the lam ever since. If he ever caught us, I could be arrested for having bootleg genes."

"Who told you that story?" he said, obviously skeptical.

"Maya did. It sounds like something one of her boyfriends would do. She has really bad taste in men. That's another reason we have to move so much."

Shaking his head slightly, he said, "I should think you would get cognitive dysplasia."

"I'm used to it," Thorn said.

"Do you like it?"

No one had ever asked her that before, as if she was capable of deciding for herself. In fact, she had known for a while that she *didn't* like it much. With every jump between planets she had grown more and more reluctant to leave sequential time behind. She said, "The worst thing is, there's no way of going back. Once you leave, the place you've stepped out of is gone forever. When I was eight I learned about pepcies, that you can use them to communicate instantaneously, and I asked Maya if we could call up my best friend on the last planet, and Maya said, 'She'll be middle-aged by now.' Everyone else had changed, and I hadn't. For a while I had dreams that the world was dissolving behind my back whenever I looked away."

The old man was listening thoughtfully, studying her. "How did you get away from Gmintagad?" he asked.

"We had Capellan passports," Thorn said. "I don't remember much about it; I was just four years old. I remember drooping cypress trees and rushing to get out. I didn't understand what was happening."

He was staring into the distance, focused on something invisible. Suddenly, he got up as if something had bitten him and started to walk away.

"Wait!" Thorn called. "What's the matter?"

He stopped, his whole body tense, then turned back. "Meet me here at four hours forenote tomorrow, if you want lessons," he said. "Bring a slate. I won't wait for you." He turned away again.

"Stop!" Thorn said. "What's your name?"

With a forbidding frown, he said, "Soren Pregaldin. You may call me Magister."

"Yes, Magister," Thorn said, trying not to let her glee show. She could hardly wait to tell Hunter that she had followed his advice, and succeeded.

What she wouldn't tell him, she decided as she watched Magister Pregaldin stalk away across the park, was her suspicion that this man knew something about the Holocide. Otherwise, how would he have known it was exactly 141 years ago? Another person would have said 140, or something else vague. She would not mention her suspicion to Hunter until she was sure. She would investigate carefully, like a competent field agent should. Thinking about it, a thrill ran through her. What if she were able to catch a Gminta? How impressed Hunter would be! The truth was, she wanted to impress Hunter. For all his mordant manner, he was by far the smartest boyfriend Maya had taken up with, the only one with a profession Thorn had ever been able to admire.

She fastened the veil over her face again before going home, so no one would see her grinning.

Magister Pregaldin turned out to be the most demanding teacher Thorn had ever known. Always before, she had coasted through school, easily able to stay ahead of the indigenous students around her, always waiting in boredom for them to catch up. With Magister Pregaldin there was no one else to wait for, and he pushed her mercilessly to the edge of her abilities. For the first time in her life, she wondered if she were smart enough.

He was an exacting drillmaster in mathematics. Once, when she complained at how useless it was, he pointed out beyond the iron gridwork of the dome to a round black hill that was conspicuous on the red plain of the crater bed. "Tell me how far away the Creeping Ingot is."

The Creeping Ingot had first come across the horizon almost a hundred years before, slowly moving toward Glory to God. It was a near-pure lump of iron the size of a small mountain. In the Waste, the reigning

theory was that it was molten underneath, and moving like a drop of wa-
ter skitters across a hot frying pan. In the city above them, it was regarded
as a sign of divine wrath: a visible, unstoppable Armageddon. Religious
tourists came from all over the planet to see it, and its ever-shrinking
distance was posted on the public sites. Thorn turned to her slate to look
it up, but Magister Pregaldin made her put it down. "No," he said, "I want
you to figure it out."

"How can I?" she said. "They bounce lasers off it or something to find
out where it is."

"There is an easier way, using tools you already have."

"The *easiest* way is to look it up!"

"No, that is the lazy way." His face looked severe. "Relying too much on
free information makes you as vulnerable as relying too much on technol-
ogy. You should always know how to figure it out yourself, because information can be falsified, or taken away. You should never trust it."

So he was some sort of information survivalist. "Next you'll want me
to use flint to make fire," she grumbled.

"Thinking for yourself is not obsolete. Now, how are you going to find
out? I will give you a hint: you don't have enough information right now.
Where are you going to get it?"

She thought a while. It had to use mathematics, because that was what
they had been talking about. At last she said, "I'll need a tape measure."

"Right."

"And a protractor."

"Good. Now go do it."

It took her the rest of forenote to assemble her tools, and the first part
of afternote to observe the ingot from two spots on opposite ends of the
park. Then she got one of the refuse-picker children to help her measure
the distance between her observation posts. Armed with two angles and
a length, the trigonometry was simple. When Magister Pregaldin let her
check her answer, it was more accurate than she had expected.

He didn't let on, but she could tell that he was, if anything, even more
pleased with her success than she was herself. "Good," he said. "Now, if
you measured more carefully and still got an answer different from the
official one, you would have to ask yourself whether the Protectorate had
a reason for falsifying the Ingot's distance."

She could see now what he meant.

"That old Vind must be a wizard," Hunter said when he found Thorn
toiling over a math problem at the kitchen table. "He's figured out some
way of motivating you."

"Why do you think he's a Vind?" Thorn said.

Hunter gave a caustic laugh. "Just look at him."

She silently added that to her mental dossier on her tutor. Not a Gminta, then. A Vind—one of the secretive race of aristocrat intellectuals who could be found in government, finance, and academic posts on almost every one of the Twenty Planets. All her life Thorn had heard whispers about a Vind conspiracy to infiltrate positions of power under the guise of public service. She had heard about the secret Vind sodality of interplanetary financiers who siphoned off the wealth of whole planets to fund their hegemony. She knew Maya scoffed at all of it. Certainly, if Magister Pregaldin was an example, the Vind conspiracy was not working very well. He seemed as penniless as any other Waster.

But being Vind did not rule out his involvement in the Holocide—it just meant he was more likely to have been a refugee than a perpetrator. Like most planets, Gmintagad had had a small, elite Vind community, regarded with suspicion by the indigenes. The massacres had targeted the Vinds as well as the Alloes. People didn't talk as much about the Vinds, perhaps because the Vinds didn't talk about it themselves.

Inevitably, Thorn's daily lessons in the park drew attention. One day they were conducting experiments in aerodynamics with paper airplanes when a man approached them. He had a braided beard strung with ceramic beads that clacked as he walked. Magister Pregaldin saw him first, and his face went blank and inscrutable.

The clatter of beads came to rest against the visitor's silk kameez. He cleared his throat. Thorn's tutor stood and touched his earlobes in respect, as people did on this planet. "Your worship's presence makes my body glad," he said formally.

The man made no effort to be courteous in return. "Do you have a license for this activity?"

"Which activity, your worship?"

"Teaching in a public place."

Magister Pregaldin hesitated. "I had no idea my conversations could be construed as teaching."

It was the wrong answer. Even Thorn, watching silently, could see that the proper response would have been to ask how much a license cost. The man was obviously fishing for a bribe. His face grew stern. "Our blessed Protectorate levies just fines on those who flout its laws."

"I obey all the laws, honorable sir. I will cease to give offense immediately."

The magister picked up his battered old electronic slate and, without a glance at Thorn, walked away. The man from the Protectorate considered Thorn, but evidently concluded he couldn't extract anything from her, and so he left.

Thorn waited till the official couldn't see her anymore, then sprinted after Magister Pregaldin. He had disappeared into Weezer Alley, a crooked passageway that Thorn ordinarily avoided because it was the epicenter of depravity in the Waste. She plunged into it now, searching for the tall, patrician silhouette of her tutor. It was still forenote, and the denizens of Weezer Alley were just beginning to rise from catering to the debaucheries of yesternote's customers. Thorn hurried past a shop where the owner was beginning to lay out an array of embarrassingly explicit sex toys; she tried not to look. A little beyond, she squeamishly skirted a spot where a shopkeeper was scattering red dirt on a half-dried pool of vomit. Several dogleg turns into the heart of the sin warren, she came to the infamous Garden of Delights, where live musicians were said to perform. No one from the Protectorate cared much about prostitution, since that was mentioned in their holy book; but music was absolutely forbidden.

The gate into the Garden of Delights was twined about with iron snakes. On either side of it stood a pedestal where dancers gyrated during open hours. Now a sleepy she-man lounged on one of them, stark naked except for a bikini that didn't hide much. Hisher smooth skin was almost completely covered with the vinelike and paisley patterns of the decorative skin fungus *mycochromoderm*. Once injected, it was impossible to remove. It grew as long as its host lived, in bright scrolls and branching patterns. It had been a Waster fad once.

The dancer regarded Thorn from lizardlike eye slits in a face forested over with green and red tendrils. "You looking for the professor?" heshe asked.

Thorn was a little shocked that her cultivated tutor was known to such an exhibitionist creature as this, but she nodded. The she-man gestured languidly at a second-story window across the street. "Tell him to come visit me," heshe said, and bared startlingly white teeth.

Thorn found the narrow doorway almost hidden behind an awning and climbed the staircase past peeling tin panels that once had shown houris carrying a huge feather fan. When she knocked on the door at the top, there was no response at first, so she called out, "Magister?"

The door flew open and Magister Pregaldin took her by the arm and yanked her in, looking to make sure she had not been followed. "What are you doing here?" he demanded.

"No one saw me," she said. "Well, except for that…that.…" She gestured across the street.

Magister Pregaldin went to the window and looked out. "Oh, Ginko," he said.

"Why do you live here?" Thorn said. "There are lots better places."

The magister gave a brief, grim little smile. "Early warning system," he said. "As long as the Garden is allowed to stay in business, no one is going to care about the likes of me." He frowned sternly. "Unless you get me in trouble."

"Why didn't you bribe him? He would have gone away."

"I have to save my bribes for better causes," he said. "One can't become known to the bottom-feeders, or they get greedy." He glanced out the window again. "You have to leave now."

"Why?" she said. "All he said was you need a license to teach in public. He didn't say anything about teaching in private."

Magister Pregaldin regarded her with a complex expression, as if he were trying to quantify the risk she represented. At last he gave a nervous shrug. "You must promise not to tell anyone. I am serious. This is not a game."

"I promise," Thorn said.

She had a chance then to look around. Up to now, her impression had been of a place so cluttered that only narrow lanes were left to move about the room. Now she saw that the teetering stacks all around her were constructed of wondrous things. There were crystal globes on ormolu stands, hand-knotted silk rugs piled ten high, clocks with malachite cases stacked atop towers of leather-and-gilt books. There was a copper orrery of nested bands and onyx horses rearing on their back legs, and a theremin in a case of brushed aluminum. A cloisonné ewer as tall as Thorn occupied one corner. In the middle hung a chandelier that dripped topaz swags and bangles, positioned so that Magister Pregaldin had to duck whenever he crossed the room.

"Is all this stuff yours?" Thorn said, dazzled with so much wonder.

"Temporarily," he said. "I am an art dealer. I make sure things of beauty get from those who do not appreciate them to those who do. I am a matchmaker, in a way." As he spoke, his fingers lightly caressed a sculpture made from an ammonite fossil with a human face emerging from the shell. It was a delicate gesture, full of reverence, even love. Thorn had a sudden, vivid feeling that this was where Magister Pregaldin's soul rested—with his things of beauty.

"If you are to come here, you must never break anything," he said.

"I won't touch," Thorn said.

"No, that's not what I meant. One *must* touch things, and hold them, and work them. Mere looking is never enough. But touch them as they wish to be touched." He handed her the ammonite fossil. Its curve fit perfectly in her hand. The face looked surprised when she held it up before her, and she laughed.

Most of the walls were as crowded as the floor, with paintings hung against overlapping tapestries and guidons. But one wall was empty except for a painting that hung alone, as if in a place of honor. As Thorn walked toward it, it seemed to shift and change colors with every change of angle. It showed a young girl with long black hair and a serious expression, about Thorn's age but far more beautiful and fragile.

Seeing where she was looking, Magister Pregaldin said, "The portrait is made of butterfly wings. It is a type of artwork from Vindahar."

"Is that the home world of the Vind?"

"Yes."

"Do you know who she is?"

"Yes," he said hesitantly. "But it would mean nothing to you. She died a long time ago."

There was something in his voice—was it pain? No, Thorn decided, something less acute, like the memory of pain. It lay in the air after he stopped speaking, till even he heard it.

"That is enough art history for today," he said briskly. "We were speaking of airplanes."

That afternote, Hunter was out on one of his inscrutable errands. Thorn waited till Maya was talking to one of her friends and crept up to Hunter's office. He had a better library than anyone she had ever met, a necessary thing on this planet where there were almost no public sources of knowledge. Thorn was quite certain she had seen some art books in his collection. She scanned the shelves of disks and finally took down one that looked like an art encyclopedia. She inserted it into the reader and typed in "butterfly" and "Vindahar."

There was a short article from which she learned that the art of butterfly-wing painting had been highly admired, but was no longer practiced because the butterflies had gone extinct. She went on to the illustrations— and there it was. The very same painting she had seen earlier that day, except lit differently, so that the colors were far brighter and the girl's expression even sadder than it had seemed.

Portrait of Jemma Diwali, the caption said. *An acknowledged masterpiece of technique, this painting was lost in GM 862, when it was looted from one of the homes of the Diwali family. According to Almasy, the representational formalism of the subject is subtly circumvented by the transformational perspective, which creates an abstractionist counter-layer of imagery. It anticipates the "chaos art" of Dunleavy....* It went on about the painting as if it had no connection to anything but art theory. But all Thorn cared about was the first sentence. GM 862—the year of the Gmintan Holocide.

Jemma was staring at her gravely, as if there were some implied expectation on her mind. Thorn went back to the shelves, this time for a history of the Holocide. It seemed like there were hundreds of them. At last she picked one almost at random and typed in "Diwali." There were uninformative references to the name scattered throughout the book. From the first two, she gathered that the Diwalis had been a Vind family associated with the government on Gmintagad. There were no mentions of Jemma.

She had left the door ajar and now heard the sounds of Hunter returning downstairs. Quickly she re-cased the books and erased her trail from the reader. She did not want him to find out just yet. This was her mystery to solve.

There wasn't another chance to sneak into Hunter's office before she returned to Magister Pregaldin's apartment on Weezer Alley. She found that he had cleared a table for them to work at, directly underneath the stuffed head of a creature with curling copper-colored horns. As he checked over the work she had done the note before, her eyes were drawn irresistibly to the portrait of Jemma across the room.

At last he caught her staring at it, and their eyes met. She blurted out, "Did you know that painting comes from Gmintagad?"

A shadow of frost crossed his face. But it passed quickly, and his voice was low and even when he said, "Yes."

"It was looted," Thorn said. "Everyone thought it was lost."

"Yes, I know," he said.

Accusatory thoughts were bombarding her. He must have seen them, for he said calmly, "I collect art from the Holocide."

"That's macabre," she said.

"A great deal of significant art was looted in the Holocide. In the years after, it was scattered, and entered the black markets of a dozen planets. Much of it was lost. I am reassembling a small portion of it, whatever I can rescue. It is very slow work."

This explanation altered the picture Thorn had been creating in her head. Before, she had seen him as a scavenger feeding on the remains of a tragedy. Now he seemed more like a memorialist acting in tribute to the dead. Regretting what she had been thinking, she said, "Where do you find it?"

"In curio shops, import stores, estate sales. Most people don't recognize it. There are dealers who specialize in it, but I don't talk to them."

"Don't you think it should go back to the families that owned it?"

He hesitated a fraction of a second, then said, "Yes, I do." He glanced over his shoulder at Jemma's portrait. "If one of them existed, I would give it back."

"You mean they're *all* dead? Every one of them?"

"So far as I can find out."

That gave the artwork a new quality. To its delicacy, its frozen-flower beauty, was added an iron frame of absolute mortality. An entire family, vanished. Thorn got up to go look at it, unable to stay away.

"The butterflies are all gone, too," she said.

Magister Pregaldin came up behind her, looking at the painting as well. "Yes," he said. "The butterflies, the girl, the family, the world, all gone. It can never be replicated."

There was something exquisitely poignant about the painting now. The only surviving thing to prove that they had all existed. She looked up at Magister Pregaldin. "Were you there?"

He shook his head slowly. "No. It was before my time. I have always been interested in it, that's all."

"Her name was Jemma," Thorn said. "Jemma Diwali."

"How did you find that out?" he asked.

"It was in a book. A stupid book. It was all about abstractionist counter-layers and things. Nothing that really explained the painting."

"I'll show you what it was talking about," the magister said. "Stand right there." He positioned her about four feet from the painting, then took the lamp and moved it to one side. As the light moved, the image of Jemma Diwali disappeared, and in its place was an abstract design of interlocking spirals, spinning pinwheels of purple and blue.

Thorn gave an exclamation of astonishment. "How did that happen?"

"It is in the microscopic structure of the butterfly wings," Magister Pregaldin explained. "Later, I will show you one under magnification. From most angles they reflect certain wavelengths of light, but from this one, they reflect another. The skill in the painting was assembling them so they would show both images. Most people think it was just a feat of technical virtuosity, without any meaning."

She looked at him. "But that's not what you think."

"No," he said. "You have to understand, Vind art is all about hidden messages, layers of meaning, riddles to be solved. Since I have had the painting here, I have been studying it, and I have identified this pattern. It was not chosen randomly." He went to his terminal and called up a file. A simple algebraic equation flashed onto the screen. "You solve this equation using any random number for X, then take the solution and use it as X to solve the equation again, then take *that* number and use it to solve the equation again, and so forth. Then you graph all the solutions on an X and Y axis, and this is what you get." He hit a key and an empty graph appeared on the screen. As the machine started to solve the equation, little dots of blue began appearing in random locations on the screen. There appeared to be no pattern at all, and Thorn frowned in perplexity.

"I'll speed it up now," Magister Pregaldin said. The dots started appearing rapidly, like sleet against a window or sand scattered on the floor. "It is like graphing the result of a thousand dice throws, sometimes lucky, sometimes outside the limits of reality, just like the choices of a life. You spend the first years buffeted by randomness, pulled this way by parents, that way by friends, all the variables squabbling and nudging, quarreling till you can't hear your own mind. And then, patterns start to appear."

On the screen, the dots had started to show a tendency to cluster. Thorn could see the hazy outlines of spiral swirls. As more and more dots appeared in seemingly random locations, the pattern became clearer and clearer.

Magister Pregaldin said, "As the pattern fills in, you begin to see that the individual dots were actually the pointillist elements of something beautiful: a snowflake, or a spiral, or concentric ripples. There is a pattern to our lives; we just experience it out of order, and don't have enough data at first to see the design. Our path forward is determined by this invisible artwork, the creation of a lifetime of events."

"You mean, like fate?" Thorn said.

"That is the question." Her tutor nodded gravely, staring at the screen. The light made his face look planar and secretive. "Does the pattern exist before us? Is our underlying equation predetermined, or is it generated by the results of our first random choice for the value of X? I can't answer that."

The pattern on the screen was clear now; it was the same one hidden under the portrait. Thorn glanced from one to the other. "What does this have to do with Jemma?"

"Another good question," Magister Pregaldin said thoughtfully. "I don't know. Perhaps it was a message to her from the artist, or a prediction— one that never had a chance to come true, because she died before she could find her pattern."

Thorn was silent a moment, thinking of that other girl. "Did she die in the Holocide?"

"Yes."

"Did you know her?"

"I told you, I wasn't there."

She didn't believe him for a second. He *had* been there, she was sure of it now. Not only had he been there, he was still there, and would always be there.

Several days later Thorn stepped out of the front door on her way to classes, and instantly sensed something wrong. There was a hush; tension or expectation had stretched the air tight. Too few people were on the street, and they were casting glances up at the city. She looked up toward where the Corkscrew rose, a black sheet-iron spiral that looked poised to drill a hole through the sky. There was a low, rhythmic sound coming from around it.

"Bick!" she cried out when she saw the Waster heading home laden down with groceries, as if for a siege. "What's going on?"

"You haven't heard?" Bick said.

"No."

In a low voice, Bick said, "The Protector was assassinated last note."

"Oh. Is that good or bad?"

Bick shrugged. "It depends on who they blame."

As Bick hurried on her way, Thorn stood, balanced between going home and going on to warn Magister Pregaldin. The sound from above grew more distinct, as of slow drumming. Deciding abruptly, Thorn dashed on.

The denizens of Weezer Alley had become accustomed to the sight of Thorn passing through to her lessons. Few of them were abroad this forenote, but she nearly collided with one coming out of the tobacco shop.

It was a renegade priest from Glory to God who had adopted the Waster lifestyle as if it were his own. Everyone called him Father Sin.

"Ah, girl!" he exclaimed. "So eager for knowledge you knock down old men?"

"Father Sin, what's that sound?" she asked.

"They are beating the doorways of their houses in grief," he said. "It is tragic, what has happened."

She dashed on. The sound had become a ringing by the time she reached Magister Pregaldin's doorway, like an unnatural Note. She had to wait several seconds after knocking before the door opened.

"Ah, Thorn! I am glad you are here," Magister Pregaldin said when he saw her. "I have something I need to...." He stopped, seeing her expression. "What is wrong?"

"Haven't you heard the news, Magister?"

"What news?"

"The Protector is dead. Assassinated. That's what the ringing is about."

He listened as if noticing it for the first time, then quickly went to his terminal to look up the news. There was a stark announcement from the Protectorate, blaming "Enemies of God," but of course no news. He shut it off and stood thinking. Then he seemed to come to a decision.

"This should not alter my plans," he said. "In fact, it may help." He turned to Thorn, calm and austere as usual. "I need to make a short journey. I will be away for two days, three at most. But if it takes me any longer, I will need you to check on my apartment, and make sure everything is in order. Will you do that?"

"Of course," Thorn said. "Where are you going?"

"I'm taking the wayport to one of the other city-states." He began then to show her two plants that would need watering, and a bucket under a leaky pipe that would need to be emptied. He paused at the entrance to his bedroom, then finally gestured her in. It was just as cluttered as the other rooms. He took a rug off a box, and she saw that it was actually a small refrigerator unit with a temperature gauge on the front showing that the interior was well below freezing.

"This needs to remain cold," he said. "If the electricity should go out, it will be fine for up to three days. But if I am delayed getting back, and the inside temperature starts rising, you will need to go out and get some dry ice to cool it again. Here is the lock. Do you remember the recursive equation I showed you?"

"You mean Jemma's equation?"

He hesitated in surprise, then said, "Yes. If you take twenty-seven for the first value of X, then solve it five times, that will give you the combination. That should be child's play for you."

"What's in it?" Thorn asked.

At first he seemed reluctant to answer, but then realized he had just given her the combination, so he knelt and pecked it out on the keypad. A light changed to green. He undid several latches and opened the top, then removed an ice pack and stood back for her to see. Thorn peered in and saw nested in ice a ball of white feathers.

"It's a bird," she said in puzzlement.

"You have seen birds, have you?"

"Yes. They don't have them here. Why are you keeping a dead bird?"

"It's not dead," he said. "It's sleeping. It is from a species they call ice owls, the only birds known to hibernate. They are native to a planet called Ping, where the winters last a century or more. The owls burrow into the ice to wait out the winter. Their bodies actually freeze solid. Then when spring comes, they revive and rise up to mate and produce the next generation."

The temperature gauge had gone yellow, so he fitted the ice pack back in place and latched the top. The refrigerator hummed, restoring the chest to its previous temperature.

"There was a…I suppose you would call it a fad, once, for keeping ice owls. When another person came along with a suitable owl, the owners would allow them both to thaw so they could come back to life and mate. It was a long time ago, though. I don't know whether there are still any freezer owls alive but this one."

Another thing that might be the last of its kind. This apartment was full of reminders of extinction, as if Magister Pregaldin could not free his mind of the thought.

But this one struck Thorn differently, because the final tragedy had not taken place. There was still a hope of life. "I'll keep it safe," she promised gravely.

He smiled at her. It made him look strangely sad. "You are a little like an owl yourself," he said kindly. "Older than the years you have lived."

She thought, but did not say, that he was also like an owl—frozen for 141 years.

They left the apartment together, she heading for home and he with a backpack over his shoulder, bound for the waystation.

Thorn did not wait two days to revisit the apartment alone to do some true detective work.

It was the day of the Protector's funeral, and Glory to God was holding its breath in pious suspension. All businesses were closed, even in the Waste, while the mourning rituals went on. Whatever repercussions would come from the assassination, they would not occur this day. Still, Thorn wore the veil when she went out, because it gave her a feeling of invisibility.

The magister's apartment was very quiet and motionless when she let herself in. She checked on the plants and emptied the pail in order to give her presence the appearance of legitimacy. She then went into the magister's bedroom, ostensibly to check the freezer, but really to look around, for she had only been in there the one time. She studied the art-encrusted walls, the shaving mirror supported by mythical beasts, the armoire full of clothes that had once been fine but now were shabby and outmoded. As she was about to leave she spotted a large box—a hexagonal column about three feet tall—on a table in a corner. It was clearly an offworld artifact because it was made of wood. Many sorts of wood, actually: the surface was an inlaid honeycomb design. But there were no drawers, no cabinets, no way inside at all. Thorn immediately realized that it must be a puzzle box—and she wanted to get inside.

She felt all around it for sliding panels, levers, or springs, but could not find any, so she brought over a lamp to study it. The surface was a parquet of hexagons, but the colors were not arranged in a regular pattern. Most tiles were made from a blond-colored wood and a reddish wood, interrupted at irregular intervals by hexagons of chocolate, caramel, and black. It gave her the strong impression of a code or diagram, but she could not imagine what sort.

It occurred to her that perhaps she was making this more complex than necessary, and the top might come off. So she tried to lift it—and indeed it shifted up, but only about an inch, enough to disengage the top row of hexagons from the ones below. In that position she found she could turn the lower rows. Apparently, it was like a cylinder padlock. Each row of hexagons was a tumbler that needed to be turned and aligned correctly for the box to open. She did not have the combination, but knowing the way Magister Pregaldin's Vind mind worked, she felt sure that there would be some hint, some way to figure it out.

Once more she studied the honeycomb inlay. There were six rows. The top one was most regular—six blond hexagons followed by six red hexagons, repeating around the circumference of the box. The patterns became more colorful in the lower rows, but always included the repeating line of six blond hexagons. For a while she experimented with spinning the rows to see if she could hit on something randomly, but soon gave up. Instead, she fetched her slate from her backpack and photographed the box, shifting it on the table to get the back. When she was done, she found that the top would no longer lock down in its original position. The instant Magister Pregaldin saw it, he would know that she had raised it. It was evidently meant as a tamper detector, and she had set it off. Now she needed to solve the puzzle, or explain to him why she had been prowling his apartment looking for evidence.

She walked home preoccupied. The puzzle was clearly about sixes—six sides, six rows, six hexagons in a row. She needed to think of formulas that involved sixes. When she reached home she went to her room and started transferring the box's pattern from the photos to a diagram so she could see it better. All that afternote she worked on it, trying to find algorithms that would produce the patterns she saw. Nothing seemed to work. The thought that she would fail, and have to confess to Magister Pregaldin, made her feeling of urgency grow. The anticipation of his disappointment and lost trust kept her up long after she should have pulled the curtains against the perpetual sun and gone to bed.

At about six hours forenote a strange dream came to her. She was standing before a tree whose trunk was a hexagonal pillar, and around it was twined a snake with Magister Pregaldin's eyes. It looked at her mockingly, then took its tail in its mouth.

She woke with the dream vivid in her mind. Lying there thinking, she remembered a story he had told her, about some Capellan magister named Kekule, who had deduced the ringlike structure of benzene after dreaming of a snake. She smiled with the thought that she had just had Kekule's dream.

Then she bounded out of bed and out her door, pounding down the spiral steps to the kitchen. Hunter and Maya were eating breakfast together when she erupted into the room.

"Hunter! Do you have any books on chemistry?" she said.

He regarded her as if she were demented. "Why?"

"I need to know about benzene!"

The two adults looked at each other, mystified. "I have an encyclopedia," he said.

"Can I go borrow it?"

"No. I'll find it for you. Now try to curb your enthusiasm for aromatic hydrocarbons till I've had my coffee."

He sat there tormenting her for ten minutes till he was ready to go up to his office and find the book for her. She took the disk saying, "Thanks, you're the best!" and flew upstairs with it. As soon as she found the entry on benzene her hunch was confirmed: it was a hexagonal ring of carbon atoms with hydrogens attached at the corners. By replacing hydrogens with different molecules you could create a bewildering variety of compounds.

So perhaps the formula she should have been looking for was not a mathematical one, but a chemical one. When she saw the diagrams for toluene, xylene, and mesitylene she began to see how it might work. Each compound was constructed from a benzene ring with methyl groups attached in different positions. Perhaps, then, each ring on the box represented a different compound and the objective was to somehow align the corners as they were shown in the diagrams. But which compounds?

Then the code of the inlaid woods came clear to her. The blond-colored hexagons were carbons, the red ones were hydrogens. The other colors probably stood for elements like nitrogen or oxygen. The chemical formulae were written right on the box for all to see.

After an hour of scribbling and looking up formulae, she was racing down the steps again with her solutions in her backpack. She grabbed a pastry from the kitchen and ate it on her way, praying that Magister Pregaldin would not have returned.

He had not. The apartment still seemed to be dozing in its emptiness. She went straight to the box. As she dialed each row to line up the corners properly, her excitement grew. When the last ring slid into place, a vertical crack appeared along one edge. The sides swung open on hinges to reveal compartments inside.

There were no gold or rubies, just papers. She took one from its slot and unfolded it. It was an intricate diagram composed of spidery lines connecting geometric shapes with numbers inside, as if to show relationships or pathways. There was no key, nor even a word written on it. The next one she looked at was all words, closely written to the very edges of the paper in a tiny, obsessive hand. In some places they seemed to be telling a surreal story about angels, magic papayas, and polar magnetism; in others they disintegrated into garbled nonsense. The next document was a map of sorts, with coastlines and roads inked in, and landmarks given allegorical names like Perfidy, Imbroglio, and Redemption Denied. The next was a complex chart of concentric circles divided into sections and labeled in an alphabet she had never seen before.

Either Magister Pregaldin was a madman or he was trying to keep track of something so secret that it had to be hidden under multiple layers of code. Thorn spread out each paper on the floor and took a picture of it, then returned it to its pigeonhole so she could puzzle over them at leisure. When she was done she closed the box and spun the rings to randomize them again. Now she could push the top back down and lock it in place.

She walked home a little disappointed, but feeling as if she had learned something about her tutor. There was an obsessive and paranoid quality about the papers that ill fitted the controlled and rational magister. Clearly, there were more layers to him than she had guessed.

When she got home, she trudged up the stairs to return the encyclopedia to Hunter. As she was raising her hand to knock on his office door, she heard a profane exclamation from within. Then Hunter came rocketing out. Without a glance at Thorn he shot down the stairs to the kitchen.

Thorn followed. He was brewing coffee and pacing. She sat on the steps and said, "What's the matter?"

He glanced up, shook his head, then it boiled out: "One of the suspects I have been following was murdered last night."

"Really?" So he *did* know of Gmintas in hiding. Or had known. Thinking it over, she said, "I guess it was a good time for a murder, in the middle of the mourning."

"It didn't happen here," he said irritably. "It was in Flaming Sword of Righteousness. Damn! We were days away from moving in on him. We had all the evidence to put him on trial before the Court of a Thousand Peoples. Now all that work has gone to waste."

She watched him pour coffee, then said, "What would have happened if the Court found him guilty?"

"He would have been executed," Hunter said. "There is not the slightest doubt. He was one of the worst. We've wanted him for decades. Now we'll never have justice; all we've got is revenge."

Thorn sat quiet then, thinking about justice and revenge, and why one was so right and the other so wrong, when they brought about the same result. "Who did it?" she asked at last.

"If I knew I'd track him down," Hunter said darkly.

He started back up the stairs with his coffee, and she had to move aside for him. "Hunter, why do you care so much about such an old crime?" she asked. "There are so many bad things going on today that need fixing."

He looked at her with a tight, unyielding expression. "To forget is to condone," he said. "Evil must know it will pay. No matter how long it takes."

"He's such a phony," she said to Magister Pregaldin the next day.

She had returned to his apartment that morning to find everything as usual, except for a half-unpacked crate of new artworks in the middle of the living room. They had sat down to resume lessons as if nothing had changed, but neither of them could concentrate on differential equations. So Thorn told him about her conversation with Hunter.

"What really made him mad was that someone beat him," Thorn said. "It's not really about justice, it's about competition. He wants the glory of having bagged a notorious Gminta. That's why it has to be public. I guess that's the difference between justice and revenge: when it's justice somebody gets the credit."

Magister Pregaldin had been listening thoughtfully; now he said, "You are far too cynical for someone your age."

"Well, people are disappointing!" Thorn said.

"Yes, but they are also complicated. I would wager there is something about him you do not know. It is the only thing we can ever say about people with absolute certainty: that we don't know the whole story."

It struck Thorn that what he said was truer of him than of Hunter.

He rose from the table and said, "I want to give you a gift, Thorn. We'll call it our lesson for the day."

Intrigued, she followed him into his bedroom. He took the rug off the freezer and checked the temperature, then unplugged it. He then took a small two-wheeled dolly from a corner and tipped the freezer onto it.

"You're giving me the ice owl?" Thorn said in astonishment.

"Yes. It is better for you to have it; you are more likely than I to meet someone else with another one. All you have to do is keep it cold. Can you do that?"

"Yes!" Thorn said eagerly. She had never owned something precious, something unique. She had never even had a pet. She was awed by the fact that Magister Pregaldin would give her something he obviously prized so much. "No one has ever trusted me like this," she said.

"Well, you have trusted me," he murmured without looking. "I need to return some of the burden."

He helped her get it down the steps. Once onto the street, she was able to wheel it by herself. But before leaving, she threw her arms giddily around her tutor and said, "Thank you, Magister! You're the best teacher I've ever had."

Wheeling the freezer through the alley, she attracted the attention of some young Wasters lounging in front of a betel parlor, who called out loudly to ask if she had a private stash of beer in there, and if they could have some. When she scowled and didn't answer they laughed and called her a lush. By the time she got home, her exaltation had been jostled aside by disgust and fury at the place where she lived. She managed to wrestle the freezer up the stoop and over the threshold into the kitchen, but when she faced the narrow spiral stair, she knew this was as far as she could get without help. The kitchen was already crowded, and the only place she could fit the freezer in was under the table. As she was shoving it against the wall, Maya came down the stairs and said, "What are you doing?"

"I have to keep this freezer here," Thorn said.

"You can't put it there. It's not convenient."

"Will you help me carry it up to my room?"

"You're kidding."

"I didn't think so. Then it's got to stay here."

Maya rolled her eyes at the irrational acts of teenagers. Now Thorn was angry at her, too. "It has to stay plugged in," Thorn said strictly. "Do you think you can remember that?"

"What's in it?"

Thorn would have enjoyed telling her if she hadn't been angry. "A science experiment," she said curtly.

"Oh, I see. None of my business, right?"

"Right."

"Okay. It's a secret," Maya said in a playful tone, as if she were talking to a child. She reached out to tousle Thorn's hair, but Thorn knocked her hand away and left, taking the stairs two at a time.

In her room, Thorn gave way to rage at her unsatisfactory life. She didn't want to be a Waster anymore. She wanted to live in a house where she could have things of her own, not squat in a boyfriend's place, always one quarrel away from eviction. She wanted a life she could control. Most of all, she wanted to leave the Waste. She went to the window and looked down at the rusty ghetto below. Cynicism hung miasmatic over it, defiling everything noble and pure. The decadent sophistication left nothing unstained.

During dinner, Maya and Hunter were cross and sarcastic with each other, and Hunter ended up storming off into his office. Thorn went to her room and studied Magister Pregaldin's secret charts till the house was silent below. Then she crept down to the kitchen to check on the freezer. The temperature gauge was reassuringly low. She sat on the brick floor with her back to it, its gentle hum soothing against her spine, feeling a kinship with the owl inside. She envied it for its isolation from the dirty world. Packed away safe in ice, it was the one thing that would never grow up, never lose its innocence. One day it would come alive and erupt in glorious joy—but only if she could protect it. Even if she couldn't protect herself, there was still something she could keep safe.

As she sat there, The Note came, filling the air full and ringing through her body like a benediction. It seemed to be answering her unfocused yearning, as if the believers were right, and there really were a force looking over her, as she looked over the owl.

When she next came to Magister Pregaldin's apartment, he was busy filling the crate up again with treasures. Thorn helped him wrap artworks in packing material as he told her which planet each one came from. "Where are you sending them?" she asked.

"Offworld," he answered vaguely.

Together they lifted the lid onto the crate, and only then did Thorn see the shipping label that had brought it here. It was stamped with a burning red sword—the customs mark of the city-state Flaming Sword of Righteousness. "Is that where you were?" she said.

"Yes."

She was about to blurt out that Hunter's Gminta had been murdered there when a terrible thought seized her: What if he already knew? What if it were no coincidence?

They sat down to lessons under the head of the copper-horned beast, but Thorn was distracted. She kept looking at her tutor's large hands, so gentle when he handled his art, and wondering if they could be the hands of an assassin.

That night Hunter went out and Maya barricaded herself in her room, leaving Thorn the run of the house. She instantly let herself into Hunter's office to search for a list of Gmintas killed and brought to justice over the years. When she tried to access his files, she found they were heavily protected by password and encryption—and if she knew his personality, he probably had intrusion detectors set. So she turned again to his library of books on the Holocide. The information was scattered and fragmentary, but after a few hours she had pieced together a list of seven mysterious murders on five planets that seemed to be revenge slayings.

Up in her room again, she took out her replica of one of Magister Pregaldin's charts, the one that looked most like a tracking chart. She started by assuming that the geometric shapes meant planets and the symbols represented individual Gmintas he had been following. After an hour she gave it up—not because she couldn't make it match, but because she could never prove it. A chart for tracking Gmintas would look identical to a chart for tracking artworks. It was the perfect cover story.

She was still awake when Hunter returned. As she listened to his footsteps she thought of going downstairs and telling him of her suspicions. But uncertainty kept her in bed, restless and wondering what was the right thing to do.

There were riots in the city the next day. In the streets far above the Waste, angry mobs flowed, a turbulent tide crashing against the Protectorate troops wherever they met. The Wasters kept close to home, looking up watchfully toward the palace, listening to the rumors that ran ratlike between the buildings. Thorn spent much of the day on the roof, a self-appointed lookout. About five hours afternote, she heard a roar from above, as of many voices raised at once. There was something elemental about the sound, as if a force of nature had broken into the domed city— a human eruption, shaking the iron framework on which all their lives depended.

She went down to the front door to see if she could catch any news. Her survival instincts were alert now, and when she spotted a little group down the street, standing on a doorstep exchanging news, she sprinted toward them to hear what they knew.

"The Incorruptibles have taken the Palace," a man told her in a low voice. "The mobs are looting it now."

"Are we safe?" she asked.

He only shrugged. "For now." They all glanced down the street toward the spike-topped gates of the Waste. The barrier had never looked flimsier.

When Thorn returned home, Maya was sitting in the kitchen looking miserable. She didn't react much to the news. Thorn sat down at the table with her, bumping her knees on the freezer underneath.

"Shouldn't we start planning to leave?" Thorn said.

"I don't want to leave," Maya said, tears coming to her already-red eyes.

"I don't either," Thorn said. "But we shouldn't wait till we don't have a choice."

"Hunter will protect us," Maya said. "He knows who to pay."

Frustrated, Thorn said, "But if the Incorruptibles take over, there won't *be* anyone to pay. That's why they call themselves incorruptible."

"It won't come to that," Maya said stubbornly. "We'll be all right. You'll see."

Thorn had heard it all before. Maya always denied that anything was wrong until everything fell apart. She acted as if planning for the worst would make it happen.

The next day the city was tense but quiet. The rumors said that the Incorruptibles were still hunting down Protectorate loyalists and throwing them in jail. The nearby streets were empty except for Wasters, so Thorn judged it safe enough to go to Weezer Alley. When she entered Magister Pregaldin's place, she was stunned at the change. The apartment had been stripped of its artworks. The carpets were rolled up, the empty walls looked dented and peeling. Only Jemma's portrait still remained. Two metal crates stood in the middle of the living room, and as Thorn was taking it all in, a pair of movers arrived to carry them off to the waystation.

"You're leaving," she said to Magister Pregaldin when he came back in from supervising the movers. She was not prepared for the disappointment she felt. All this time she had been trustworthy and kept his secrets—and he had abandoned her anyway.

"I'm sorry, Thorn," he said, reading her face. "It is becoming too dangerous here. You and your mother ought to think of leaving, as well."

"Where are you going?"

He paused. "It would be better if I didn't tell you that."

"I'm not going to tell anyone."

"Forgive me. It's a habit." He studied her for a few moments, then put his hand gently on her shoulder. "Your friendship has meant more to me than you can know," he said. "I had forgotten what it was like, to inspire such pure trust."

He didn't even know she saw through him. "You're lying to me," she said. "You've been lying all along. You're not leaving because of the Incorruptibles. You're leaving because you've finished what you came here to do."

He stood motionless, his hand still on her shoulder. "What do you mean?"

"You came here to settle an old score," she said. "That's what your life is about, isn't it? Revenge for something everyone else has forgotten and you can't let go."

He withdrew his hand. "You have made some strange mistake."

"You and Hunter—I don't understand either of you. Why can't you just stop digging up the past and move on?"

For several moments he stared at her, but his eyes were shifting as if tracking things she couldn't see. When he finally spoke, his voice was very low. "I don't *choose* to remember the past. I am compelled to—it is my punishment. Or perhaps it is a disease, or an addiction. I don't know."

Taken aback at his earnestness, Thorn said, "Punishment? For what?"

"Here, sit down," he said. "I will tell you a story before we part."

They both sat at the table where he had given her so many lessons, but before he started to speak he stood up again and paced away, his hands clenching. She waited silently, and he came back to face her, and started to speak.

This is a story about a young man who lived long ago. I will call him Till. He wanted badly to live up to his family's distinguished tradition. It was a prominent family, you see; for generations they had been involved in finance, banking, and insurance. The planet where they lived was relatively primitive and poor, but Till's family felt they were helping it by attracting outside investment and extending credit. Of course, they did very well by doing good.

The government of their country had been controlled by the Alloes for years. Even though the Alloes were an ethnic minority, they were a diligent people and had prospered by collaborating with Vind businessmen like Till's family. The Alloes ruled over the majority, the Gmintas, who had less of everything—less education, less money, less power. It was an unjust situation, and when there was a mutiny in the military and the Gmintas took control, the Vinds accepted the change. Especially to younger people like Till, it seemed like a righting of many historical wrongs.

Once the Gminta army officers were in power, they started borrowing heavily to build hospitals, roads, and schools for Gminta communities, and the Vind banks were happy to make the loans. It seemed like a good way to dispel many suspicions and prejudices that throve in the ignorance of the Gminta villages. Till was on the board of his family bank, and he argued for extending credit even after the other bankers became concerned about the government's reckless fiscal policies.

One day, Till was called into the offices of the government banking regulators. Alone in a small room, they accused him of money laundering and corruption. It was completely untrue, but they had forged documents that seemed to prove it. Till realized that he faced a life in prison. He would bring shame to his entire family, unless he could strike a deal. They offered him an alternative: he could come to work for the government, as their representative to the Vind community. He readily accepted the job, and resigned from the bank.

They gave him an office and a small staff. He had an Alloe counterpart responsible for outreach to that community; and though they never spoke about it, he suspected his colleague had been recruited with similar methods. They started out distributing informational leaflets and giving tips on broadcast shows, all quite bland. But it changed when the government decided to institute a new draft policy for military service. Every young person was to give five years' mandatory service starting at eighteen. The Vinds would not be exempt.

Now, as you may know, the Vinds are pacifists and mystics, and have never served in the military of any planet. This demand by the Gminta government was unprecedented, and caused great alarm. The Vinds gathered in the halls of their Ethical Congresses to discuss what to do. Till worked tirelessly, meeting with them and explaining the perspective of the government, reminding them of the Vind principle of obeying the local law wherever they found themselves. At the same time, he managed to get the generals to promise that no Vind would be required to serve in combat, which was utterly in violation of their beliefs. With this assurance, the Vinds reluctantly agreed. And so mothers packed bags for their children and sent them off to training, urging them to call often.

Soon after, a new land policy was announced. Estates that had always belonged to the Alloes were to be redistributed among landless Gmintas. This created quite a lot of resistance; Till and his colleague kept busy giving interviews and explaining how the policy restored fairness to the land system. They became familiar to all as government spokespeople.

Then the decision was made to relocate whole neighborhoods of Alloes and Vinds so Gmintas could have better housing in the cities. Till could no longer argue about justice; now he could only tell people it was necessary to move in order to quiet the fears of the Gmintas and preserve peace.

People started to emigrate off-planet, but then the government closed down the waystations. This nearly caused a panic, and Till had to tell everyone it was merely to prevent people from taking their goods and assets offworld, thus draining the national wealth. He promised that individuals would be allowed to leave again soon, as long as they took no cash or valuables with them.

He no longer believed it himself.

It had been months since the young people had gone off to the army, and their families had heard nothing from them. Till had been telling everyone it was a period of temporary isolation, while the trainees lived in camps on the frontier to build solidarity and camaraderie. Every time he went out, he would be surrounded by anxious parents asking when they could expect to hear from their children.

Fleets of buses showed up to evacuate the Alloe and Vind families from their homes, and take them to relocation camps. Till watched his own neighborhood become a ghost town, and the certainty grew in him that the people were never coming back. One day he entered his supervisor's office unexpectedly and overheard someone saying, "…to the morti-factories." They stopped talking when they saw him.

You are probably thinking, "Why didn't he speak out? Why didn't he denounce them?" Try to imagine, in many respects life still seemed quite normal, and what he suspected was so unthinkable it seemed insane. And even if he could overcome that, there was no one to speak out to. He was alone, and he was not a very courageous person. His only chance was to stay useful to the government.

Other Vinds and Alloes who had been working alongside him started to vanish. Still the Gmintas wanted him to go on reassuring people; he did it so well. He had to hide what he suspected, to fool them into think-ing that he was fooled himself. Every day he lived in fear of hearing the knock on his door that would mean it was his time.

It was his Alloe colleague who finally broke. They rarely let the man go on air anymore; his nerves were too shattered. But one day he substituted for Till, and in the midst of a broadcast shouted out a warning: "They are killing you! It is mass murder!" That was all he got out before they cut him off.

That night, well-armed and well-organized mobs broke into the re-maining Alloe enclaves in the capital city. The government deplored the violence the next day, but suggested that the Alloes had incited it.

At that point they no longer had any need for Till. Once again, they gave him a choice: relocation or deportation. He could join his family and share their fate; or he could leave the planet. Death or life. I think I have mentioned he was not very courageous. He chose to live.

They sent him to Capella Two, a twenty-five-year journey. By the time he arrived, the entire story had traveled ahead of him by pepci, and every-thing was known. His own role was infamous. He was the vile collabora-tor who had put a benign face on the crime. He had soothed people's fears and deceived them into walking docilely to their deaths. In hindsight, it was inconceivable that he had not known what he was doing. All across the Twenty Planets, the name of Till Diwali was reviled.

He fell silent at last. Thorn sat staring at the tabletop, because she could not sort out what to think. It was all wheeling about in her mind: right and wrong, horror and sympathy, criminal and victim—all were jumbled together. Finally she said, "Was Jemma your sister?"

"I told you, I was not there," he said in a distant voice. "The man who did those things was not me."

He was sitting at the table across from her again, his hands clasped before him. Now he spoke to her directly. "Thorn, you are unitary and authentic now as you will never be again. As you pass through life, you will accumulate other selves. Always you will be a person looking back on, and separate from, the person you are now. Whenever you walk down a street, or sit on a park bench, your past selves will be sitting beside you, impossible to touch or interrogate. In the end there is a whole crowd of you wherever you go, and you feel like you will perish from the loneliness."

Thorn's whirling feelings were beginning to come to rest in a pattern, and in it horror and blame predominated. She looked up at Jemma's face and said, "She *died*. How could you do that, and walk away? It's inhuman."

He didn't react, either to admit guilt or defend his innocence. She wanted an explanation from him, and he didn't give it. "You're a monster," she said.

Still he said nothing. She got up, blind to everything but the intensity of her thoughts, and went to the door. She glanced back before leaving, and he was looking at her with an expression that was nothing like what he ought to feel—not shame, not rage, not self-loathing. Thorn slammed the door behind her and fled.

She walked around the streets of the Waste for a long time, viciously throwing stones at heaps of trash to make the rats come out. Above the buildings, the sky seemed even redder than usual, and the shadows blacker. She was furious at the magister for not being admirable. She blamed him for hiding it from her and for telling her—since, by giving her the knowledge, he had also given her a responsibility of choosing what to do.

When she got home the kitchen was empty, but she heard voices from the living room above. She was mounting the stairs when the voices rose in anger, and she froze. It was Hunter and Maya, and they were yelling at each other.

"Good God, what were you thinking?" Hunter demanded.

"She needed help. I couldn't say no."

"You knew it would bring the authorities down on us!"

"I had a responsibility—"

"What about your responsibility to me? You just didn't think. You never think; everything is impulse with you. You are the most immature and manipulative person I've ever met."

Maya's voice went wheedling. "Hunter, come on. It'll be okay."

"And what if it's not okay? What are you going to do then? Just pick up and leave the wreckage behind you? That's what you've been doing all your life—dragging that kid of yours from planet to planet, never thinking what it's doing to her. You never think what you're doing to anyone, do you? It's all just yourself. I never should have let you in here."

There were angry footsteps, and then Hunter was mounting the stairs.

"Hunter!" Maya cried after him.

Thorn waited a minute, then crept up into the living room. Maya was sitting there, looking tragic and beautiful.

"What did you do?" Thorn said.

"It doesn't matter," Maya said. "He'll get over it."

"I don't care about Hunter."

Mistaking what she meant, Maya smiled through her tears. "You know what? I don't care either." She came over and hugged Thorn tight. "I'm not really a bad mother, am I, Thorn?"

Cautiously, Thorn said, "No...."

"People just don't understand us. We're a team, right?"

Maya held out her hand for their secret finger-hook. Once it would have made Thorn smile, but she no longer felt the old solidarity against the world. She hooked fingers anyway, because she was afraid Maya would start to cry again if she didn't. Maya said, "They just don't know you. Damaged child, poppycock—you're tough as old boots. It makes me awestruck, what a survivor you are."

"I think we ought to get ready to leave," Thorn said.

Maya's face lost its false cheer. "I can't leave," she whispered.

"Why not?"

"Because I love him."

There was no sensible answer to that. So Thorn turned away to go up to her room. As she passed the closed door of Hunter's office, she paused, wondering if she should knock. Wondering if she should turn in the most notorious Gminta collaborator still alive. All those millions of dead Alloes and Vinds would get their justice, and Hunter would be famous. Then her feet continued on, even before she consciously made the decision. It was not loyalty to Magister Pregaldin, and it was not resentment of Hunter. It was because she might need that information to buy her own safety.

The sound of breaking glass woke her. She lay tense, listening to footsteps and raised voices below in the street. Then another window broke, and she got up to pull back the curtain. The sun was orange, as always, and she squinted in the glare, then raised her window and climbed out on the roof.

Below in the street, a mob of white-clad Incorruptibles was breaking windows as they passed; but their true target obviously lay deeper in the Waste. She watched till they were gone, then waited to see what would happen.

From somewhere beyond the tower fans of the park she could hear shouts and clanging, and once an avalanche-like roar, after which a cloud of dust rose from the direction of Weezer Alley. After that there was silence for a while. At last she heard chanting. Fleeing footsteps passed below. Then the wall of Incorruptibles appeared again. They were driving someone before them with improvised whips made from their belts. Thorn peered over the eaves to see more clearly and recognized their victim—Ginko, the heshe from the Garden of Delights, completely naked, both breasts and genitals exposed, with a rope around hisher neck. The whips had cut into the delicate paisley of Ginko's skin, exposing slashes of red underneath.

At a spot beneath Thorn's perch, Ginko stumbled and fell. A mass of Incorruptibles gathered round. Two of them pulled Ginko's legs apart, and a third made a jerking motion with a knife. A womanlike scream made Thorn grip the edge of her rooftop, wanting to look away. They tossed the rope over a signpost and hoisted Ginko up by the neck, choking and clawing at the noose. The body still quivered as the army marched past. When they were gone, the silence was so complete Thorn could hear the patter of blood into a pool on the pavement under the body.

On hands and knees she backed away from the edge of the roof and climbed into her bedroom. It was already stripped; everything she valued or needed was in her backpack, ready to go. She threw on some clothes and went down the stairs.

Maya, dressed in a robe, stopped her halfway. She looked scattered and panicky. "Thorn, we've got to leave," she said.

"Right now?"

"Yes. He doesn't want us here anymore. He's acting as if we're some sort of danger to him."

"Where are we going?"

"I don't know. Some other planet. Some place without men." She started to cry.

"Go get dressed," Thorn told her. "I'll bring some food." Over her shoulder she added, "Pack some clothes and money."

With her backpack in hand, Thorn raced down to the kitchen.

She was just getting out the dolly for the ice owl's refrigerator when Maya came down.

"You're not taking that, are you?" Maya said.

"Yes, I am." Thorn knelt to shift the refrigerator out from under the table, and only then noticed it wasn't running. Quickly, she checked the temperature gauge. It was in the red zone, far too high. With an anguished exclamation, she punched in the lock code and opened the top. Not a breath of cool air escaped. The ice pack on top was gurgling and liquid. She lifted it to see what was underneath.

The owl was no longer nested snugly in ice. It had shifted, tried to open its wings. There were scratches on the insulation where it had tried to peck and claw its way out. Now it lay limp, its head thrown back. Thorn sank to her knees, griefstruck before the evidence of its terrifying last minutes—revived to life only to find itself trapped in a locked chest. Even in that stifling dark, it had longed for life so much it had fought to free itself. Thorn's breath came hard and her heart labored, as if she were reliving the ice owl's death.

"Hurry up, Thorn," Maya said. "We've got to go."

Then she saw what had happened. The refrigerator cord lay on the floor, no longer attached to the wall outlet. She held it up as if it were a murder weapon. "It's unplugged," she said.

"Oh, that's right," Maya said, distracted. "I had to plug in the curling iron. I must have forgotten."

Rage rose inside Thorn like a huge bubble of compressed air. "You *forgot*?"

"I'm sorry, Thorn. I didn't know it was important."

"I *told* you it was important. This was the last ice owl anywhere. You haven't just killed this one, you've killed the entire species."

"I said I was sorry. What do you want me to do?"

Maya would never change. She would always be like this, careless and irresponsible, unable to face consequences. Tears of fury came to Thorn's eyes. She dashed them away with her hand. "You're useless," she said, climbing to her feet and picking up her pack. "You can't be trusted to take care of anything. I'm done with you. Don't bother to follow me."

Out in the street, she turned in the direction she never went, to avoid having to pass what was hanging in the street. Down a narrow alley she sprinted, past piles of stinking refuse alive with roaches, till she came to a narrow side street that doglegged into the park. On the edge of the open space she paused under a portico to scan for danger; seeing none, she dashed across, past the old men's chess tables, past the bench where she had met Magister Pregaldin, to the entrance of Weezer Alley.

Signs of the Incorruptibles' passage were everywhere. Broken glass crunched underfoot and the contents of the shops were trampled under red dirt shoeprints. When Thorn reached the Garden of Delights, the entire street looked different, for the building had been demolished. Only a monstrous pile of rubble remained, with iron girders and ribs sticking up like broken bones. A few people climbed over the ruin, looking for survivors.

The other side of the street was still standing, but Magister Pregaldin's door had been ripped from its hinges and tossed aside. Thorn dashed up the familiar stairs. The apartment looked as if it had been looted— stripped bare, not a thing of value left. She walked through the empty rooms, dreading what she might find, and finding nothing. Out on the street again, she saw a man who had often winked at her when she passed by to her lessons. "Do you know what happened to Magister Pregaldin?" she asked. "Did he get away?"

"Who?" the man said.

"Magister Pregaldin. The man who lived here."

"Oh, the old Vind. No, I don't know where he is."

So he had abandoned her as well. In all the world, there was no one trustworthy. For a moment she had a dark wish that she had exposed his secret. Then she realized she was just thinking of revenge.

Hoisting her pack to her shoulder, she set out for the waystation. She was alone now, only herself to trust.

There was a crowd in the street outside the waystation. Everyone seemed to have decided to leave the planet at once, some of them with huge piles of baggage and children. Thorn pushed her way in toward the ticket station to find out what was going on. They were still selling tickets, she saw with relief; the crowd was people waiting for their turn in the translation chamber. Checking to make sure she had her copy of Maya's credit stick, she joined the ticket line. She was back among her own kind, the rootless, migrant elite.

Where was she going? She scanned the list of destinations. She had been born on Capella Two, but had heard it was a harshly competitive place, so she decided against it. Ben was just an ice-ball world, Gammadis was too far away. It was both thrilling and frightening to have control over where she went and what she did. She was still torn by indecision when she heard someone calling, "Thorn!"

Clarity was pushing through the crowd toward her. "I'm so glad we found you," she said when she drew close. "Maya was here a little while ago, looking for you."

"Where is she now?" Thorn asked, scanning the crowd.

"She left again."

"Good," Thorn said.

"Thorn, she was frantic. She was afraid you'd get separated."

"We *are* separated," Thorn said implacably. "She can do what she wants. I'm on my own now. Where are you going, Clarity?"

Bick had come up, carrying their ticket cards. Thorn caught her hand to look at the tickets. "Alananovis," she read aloud, then looked up to find it on the directory. It was only eighteen light-years distant. "Can I come with you?"

"Not without Maya," Clarity said.

"Okay, then I'll go somewhere else."

Clarity put a hand on her arm. "Thorn, you can't just go off without Maya."

"Yes, I can. I'm old enough to be on my own. I'm sick of her, and I'm sick of her boyfriends. I want control of my life." Besides, Maya had killed the ice owl; Maya ought to suffer. It was only justice.

She had reached the head of the line. Her eye caught a name on the list, and she made a snap decision. When the ticket seller said "Where to?" she answered, "Gmintagad." She would go to see where Jemma Diwali had lived—and died.

The translation chamber on Gmintagad was like all the others she had seen over the years: sterile and anonymous. A technician led her into a waiting room till her luggage came through by the low-resolution beam. She sat feeling cross and tired, as she always did after having her molecules reassembled out of new atoms. When at last her backpack was delivered and she went on into the customs and immigration facility, she noticed a change in the air. For the first time in years she was breathing organically manufactured oxygen. She could smell the complex and decay-laden odor of an actual ecosystem. Soon she would see sky without any dome. The thought gave her an agoraphobic thrill.

She put her identity card into the reader, and after a pause it directed her to a glass-fronted booth where an immigration official in a sand-colored uniform sat behind a desk. Unlike the air, the man looked manufactured—a face with no wrinkles, defects, or stand-out features, as if they had chosen him to match a mathematical formula for facial symmetry. His hair was neatly clipped, and so, she noticed, were his nails. When she sat opposite him, she found that her chair creaked at the slightest movement. She tried to hold perfectly still.

He regarded her information on his screen, then said, "Who is your father?"

She had been prepared to say why her mother was not with her, but her father? "I don't know," she said. "Why?"

"Your records do not state his race."

His *race*? It was an antique concept she barely understood. "He was Capellan," she said.

"Capellan is not an origin. No one evolved on Capella."

"I did," Thorn stated.

He studied her without any expression at all. She tried to meet his eyes, but it began to seem confrontational, so she looked down. Her chair creaked.

"There are certain types of people we do not allow on Gmintagad," he said.

She tried to imagine what he meant. Criminals? Disease carriers? Agitators? He could see she wasn't any of those. "Wasters, you mean?" she finally ventured.

"I mean Vinds," he said.

Relieved, she said, "Oh, well that's all right, then. I'm not Vind." Creak.

"Unless you can tell me who your father was, I cannot be sure of that," he said.

She was speechless. How could a father she had never known have any bearing on who she was?

The thought that they might not let her in made her stomach knot. Her chair sent out a barrage of telegraphic signals. "I just spent thirty-two years as a lightbeam to get here," she said. "You've got to let me stay."

"We are a sovereign principality," he said calmly. "We don't *have* to let anyone stay." He paused, his eyes still on her. "You have a Vind look. Are you willing to submit to a genetic test?"

Minutes ago, her mind had seemed like syrup. Now it bubbled with alarm. In fact, she didn't *know* her father wasn't Vind. It had never mattered, so she had never cared. But here, all the things that defined her— her interests, her aptitudes, her internal doubts—none of it counted, only her racial status. She was in a place where identity was assigned, not chosen or created.

"What happens if I fail the test?" she asked.

"You will be sent back."

"And what happens if I don't take it?"

"You will be sent back."

"Then why did you even ask?"

He gave a regulation smile. If she had measured it with a ruler, it would have been perfect. She stood up, and the chair sounded like it was laughing. "All right. Where do I go?"

They took her blood and sent her into a waiting room with two doors, neither of which had a handle. As she sat there idle, the true rashness of what she had done crept up on her. It wasn't like running away on-planet. Maya didn't know where she had gone. By now, they would be different ages. Maya could be dying, or Thorn could be older than she was, before they ever found each other. It was a permanent separation. And permanent punishment for Maya.

Thorn tried to summon up the righteous anger that had propelled her only an hour and thirty-two years before. But even that slipped from her grasp. It was replaced with a clutching feeling of her own guilt. She had known Maya's shortcomings when she took the ice owl, and never bothered to safeguard against them. She had known all the accidents the world was capable of, and still she had failed to protect a creature that could not protect itself.

Now, remorse made her bleed inside. The owl had been too innocent to meet such a terrible end. Its life should have been a joyous ascent into air, and instead it had been a hellish struggle, alone and forgotten, killed by neglect. Thorn had betrayed everyone by letting the ice owl die. Magister Pregaldin, who had trusted her with his precious possession. Even, somehow, Jemma and the other victims of Till Diwali's crime—for what had she done but reenact his failure, as if to show that human beings had learned nothing? She felt as if caught in an iron-bound cycle of history, doomed to repeat what had gone before, as long as she was no better than her predecessors had been.

She covered her face with her hands, wanting to cry, but too demoralized even for that. It seemed like a self-indulgence she didn't deserve.

The door clicked and she started up at sight of a stern, rectangular woman in a uniform skirt, whose face held the hint of a sneer. Thorn braced for the news that she would have to waste another thirty-two years on a pointless journey back to Glory to God. But instead, the woman said, "There is someone here to see you."

Behind her was a familiar face that made Thorn exclaim in joy, "Clarity!"

Clarity came into the room, and Thorn embraced her in relief. "I thought you were going to Alananovis."

"We were," Clarity said, "but we decided we couldn't just stand by and let a disaster happen. I followed you, and Bick stayed behind to tell Maya where we were going."

"Oh, thank you, thank you!" Thorn cried. Now the tears that had refused to come before were running down her face. "But you gave up thirty-two years for a stupid reason."

"It wasn't stupid for us," Clarity said. "You were the stupid one."

"I know," Thorn said miserably.

Clarity was looking at her with an expression of understanding. "Thorn, most people your age are allowed some mistakes. But you're performing life without a net. You have to consider Maya. Somehow, you've gotten older than she is even though you've been traveling together. You're the steady one, the rock she leans on. These boyfriends, they're just entertainment for her. They drop her and she bounces back. But if you dropped her, her whole world would dissolve."

Thorn said, "That's not true."

"It *is* true," Clarity said.

Thorn pressed her lips together, feeling impossibly burdened. Why did *she* have to be the reliable one, the one who was never vulnerable or wounded? Why did Maya get to be the dependent one?

On the other hand, it was a comfort that she hadn't abandoned Maya as she had done to the ice owl. Maya was not a perfect mother, but neither was Thorn a perfect daughter. They were both just doing their best.

"I hate this," she said, but without conviction. "Why do I have to be responsible for her?"

"That's what love is all about," Clarity said.

"You're a busybody, Clarity," Thorn said.

Clarity squeezed her hand. "Yes. Aren't you lucky?"

The door clicked open again. Beyond the female guard's square shoulder, Thorn glimpsed a flash of honey-gold hair. "Maya!" she said.

When she saw Thorn, Maya's whole being seemed to blaze like the sun. Dodging in, she threw her arms around Thorn.

"Oh Thorn, thank heaven I found you! I was worried sick. I thought you were lost."

"It's okay, it's okay," Thorn kept saying as Maya wept and hugged her again. "But Maya, you have to tell me something."

"Anything. What?"

"Did you seduce a *Vind*?"

For a moment Maya didn't understand. Then a secretive smile grew on her face, making her look very pretty and pleased with herself. She touched Thorn's hair. "I've been meaning to tell you about that."

"Later," Bick said. "Right now, we all have tickets for Alananovis."

"That's wonderful," Maya said. "Where's Alananovis?"

"Only seven years away from here."

"Fine. It doesn't matter. Nothing matters as long as we're together."

She held out her finger for the secret finger-lock. Thorn did it with a little inward sigh. For a moment she felt as if her whole world were composed of vulnerable beings frozen in time, as if she were the only one who aged and changed.

"We're a team, right?" Maya said anxiously.

"Yeah," Thorn answered. "We're a team."

PHOENIX PICK BOOKLETS

SMALL BOOKS WITH BIG IDEAS

Carolyn Ives Gilman

The Ice Owl (Hugo/Nebula Nominee)
Arkfall (Nebula Nominee)

Nancy Kress (coming soon in Booklet Format)

Beggars in Spain (Novella, Winner Hugo & Nebula)
Act One Hugo/Nebula Nominee)

www.PhoenixPick.com